Claudia's Carnival

Written by Nadine Cowan

Illustrated by Nadine Cowan and Katie Crumpton

Collins

Chapter 1

It was the day before Notting Hill Carnival in London. Blue Mahoes, Aniyah and her cousin EJ's family restaurant, had a food stall at the carnival every year. They served delicious food and drink from Jamaica like ackee and saltfish, jerk chicken with rice and peas, fried plantains, patties with different tasty fillings and cocoa bread.

Aniyah, EJ and their friend, Olivia, were helping to load equipment into a van parked outside the restaurant.

"I love Notting Hill Carnival!" Aniyah said.

"It's the best street party in London!" EJ agreed. "I can't wait to see the parade with all the decorated floats."

Olivia nodded. "And the music, the dancing, and the *food*."

"I know the carnival means it's the end of summer, but this is my favourite time of year," Aniyah said.

Just then, Aniyah's mum arrived at the restaurant with three large boxes.

Aniyah darted over like a firework; EJ and Olivia were not too far behind.

"Watch it!" said Aniyah's dad, as a stack of plates wobbled.

"Sorry Dad," Aniyah gulped. "I just can't wait to see it!"

Aniyah's mum chuckled as she laid the boxes down on an empty table. She lifted the first box off the pile.

"This one's yours, Aniyah," she said. "And this is yours, Olivia."

"So, *this* one must be mine," said EJ, pulling the last box towards him.

4

Aniyah prised the lid off the box and pulled the magenta tissue paper out. She had every intention of unwrapping slowly, but her excitement got the better of her and the pink paper lay crumpled on the floor.

"I love it! It's even better than the photos!" Aniyah cried.

It was a Tropical Mas carnival costume, and as she held it up, the rays from the sun shone through the restaurant window and danced across the gems, causing them to sparkle brightly.

Tropical Mas was a children's carnival band and Aniyah, Olivia and EJ were all taking part. A carnival band had its own float in the parade, and this year Tropical Mas's theme was birds of the Caribbean.

"I can't wait to dress up in our costumes and dance behind the float," Aniyah said.

Ever since they could remember, Aniyah and EJ had taken part in Notting Hill Carnival, but this was Olivia's first time going in costume.

Olivia had heard the others call it "playin mas" and Aniyah had told Olivia that "mas" was short for "masquerade". They were in the Amazona section, and their costumes had green, yellow and blue feathers.

EJ was in the Hummingbird section; his costume had shimmering green and black feathers. They were going to look just like birds native to the Caribbean.

They jumped as a voice thundered from the restaurant doorway.

Chapter 2

"Those are lovely costumes!"

It was Errol, a regular customer at Blue Mahoes. He was making his way over to the queue by the counter. His long dreadlocks, which usually swung by his waist, were tucked up snug beneath a knitted hat. He was so loud, his voice always entered the restaurant before he did, and whenever he came in, it was like the sun itself had walked into the restaurant as he regaled the children with his tales.

"We've got our costumes for carnival tomorrow!
Are you going?" EJ asked him.

"Of course! I'm there every year – it's not missing me,"
chuckled Errol. "My uncle's friend Vincent was a stowaway
on a ship from Jamaica in 1954. When he arrived in Britain,
he built a sound system with an old turntable. He had all
the latest records from Jamaica, and he brought the sound
system to the United Kingdom."

"Wow," Aniyah said, impressed. "The carnival has
the *best* sound system!"

"Where I'm from in Barbados, carnival's called Crop Over!" said a woman in the queue.

"In Grenada, the island of spice, we call it Spice Mas!" said another.

"We call it Vincy Mas in Saint Vincent and the Grenadines!" said Aniyah's dad.

Aniyah looked at her costume. "They all sound like fun."

"Will we see you there tomorrow, Winston?" Aniyah's mum asked an older gentleman.

"Oh no, I haven't been in decades. I used to go when it first started – it was held in a hall back then! But it's not the same now. The young folk just want to party and make noise for no good reason. It used to be we had something to *say*," Winston said sadly.

"But if the older generation don't take part, how can you expect the youngsters to know about traditions?" Aniyah's mum replied.

EJ, Olivia and Aniyah couldn't understand why Winston was so miserable. Carnival was about fun!

EJ whispered to the girls, "Things are really busy up here, let's go downstairs to the basement and play with the games board."

The Ludi games board was a family heirloom and it wasn't just any old board. There were words etched on the side:

Roll double six or double three,
let's learn about your history.

Whenever they played the Ludi game, something amazing happened.

When Aniyah rolled a double three, a puff of iridescent smoke erupted from the board and engulfed the children. Then a tornado appeared, that formed a wormhole, and a strong force suddenly pulled them in.

The children could hear a whisper of a tune in the distance and the smell of freshly baked bread lingered in the bitter, cold air.

Aniyah breathed out a puff of cold air and rubbed her hands together.

"Look at these gloves," she said. She looked down and noticed she was also wearing a woollen coat and skirt.

"They're a little bit itchy, but these clothes don't feel too uncomfortable," said Olivia. She was wearing tapered trousers and shiny loafers.

Suddenly, both girls were hit by a flash of light.

Chapter 3

"EJ!" Aniyah shielded her eyes and looked in the direction of the flash. EJ lowered a bulky camera from his face.

"This was hanging from my neck when we arrived," he explained.

"Where are we?" Olivia asked.

A bright red double-decker bus came roaring down the road. It was the number 59.

"Oh. We must still be in London. Look at that old red phone box! Let's look around and find out *when*," said Olivia.

EJ continued to mess around with the camera, so Olivia and Aniyah looked at the shops nearby. "Some of them have boarded-up windows, but those two are open: Caribbean Bakery and Theo's Record Store."

EJ looked up. "Well, I'm hungry, so I vote for the bakery."

Olivia rolled her eyes. "We don't have any money, so let's try the record store."

Olivia and Aniyah grabbed EJ, followed the sound of the music coming from inside the shop, and stepped inside.

The shop was dimly lit, and music pounded from a speaker. There were a few people inside browsing through boxes. Olivia began to flick through the closest box before pulling out a large cardboard square with a colourful picture on the front.

"What's this?" she asked Aniyah and EJ.

"That's a calypso record! It's only one of the most popular styles of music from Trinidad," the man from behind the counter said. "You must be Claudia's trainees."

"Er, yes, that's right," EJ replied.

"I'm Theo. I write the sports column. Claudia said you might get lost. Come on, her office is upstairs."

The children looked at
each other. "Trainees? Sports column?"
Aniyah whispered.

The others shrugged.

They followed Theo as he
went through a door next to
the record shop. They went up
some narrow steps and arrived
at another door. Theo knocked,
and they heard a voice say,
"Come in!"

Theo opened
the door and ushered
the children inside.

They were in an office above the record shop. Behind a desk in the corner of the room, sat a woman in a suit jacket, her hair pulled back away from her face. She peered up from a typewriter when the children entered and smiled.

"Ah yes, welcome! I'm so glad you can come and help us at such short notice. I'm Claudia Jones, founder and editor of *The West Indian Gazette*."

EJ shook Claudia's hand. "I'm EJ and this is my cousin, Aniyah, and our friend, Olivia. We're here to help!"

"Can you tell us a bit more about what you want us to do?" Olivia asked.

"Of course. *The Gazette* is a publication for the West Indian community here in Britain. I'm arranging Britain's first ever Caribbean carnival and I need your help to prepare."

"A carnival?" Aniyah's face lit up, "At Notting Hill?"

"Yes, that's right, a carnival. But not at Notting Hill. I've arranged for it to be held indoors at King's Cross St Pancras Town Hall."

"Indoors?" Aniyah said. "But how are you going to fit a million people in a town hall?"

Claudia laughed. "A million people! Now *that* would be something! We're not planning anything quite that big."

"Is this the very first carnival Winston was talking about?" Aniyah whispered to the others.

"Maybe," Olivia whispered back.

"I see you've brought a camera, EJ. Excellent, I need a photographer," Claudia said. "The BBC will be televising the event, too."

Claudia jumped up from her desk and gave the children a tour of the office.

"This is my desk where I edit the newspaper and organise my ideas," she explained, as she shuffled some papers into a pile.

NEWS

"My colleagues work at this desk; they won't be in today so you can work here. I need you to create a flyer promoting the carnival event for the newspaper. You can use their typewriter."

Chapter 4

EJ curiously pressed down on one of the typewriter keys. "This is *not* like using a tablet," he said.

Olivia laughed. "Yeah, that's nothing like our computer at home."

Aniyah lifted the phone receiver and held it to her ear.

"I think we can work the typewriter," she said, "but I hope we don't have to use this phone!"

Aniyah and Olivia loved drawing and writing, and making a flyer was the perfect challenge for them. Aniyah sat down at the typewriter and slowly typed out text for the poster. Olivia began to sketch out some ideas with a pen, while EJ got to work on layout ideas.

"How did you come up with the idea for a carnival, Ms Jones?" Aniyah asked.

"Please, call me Claudia. Over the last decade Britain has changed so much. Now there are many more people from lots of different cultures living here. Some people aren't happy about it, and they want Britain to go back to the way it was before, when there weren't Caribbean, African, Indian or Irish communities here."

EJ picked up a newspaper from a stack and pointed to the headline. "Is that why there's been rioting in London?" he asked.

"We saw some of the shops had boarded-up windows," Olivia added.

Claudia sighed. "Yes, there's been fighting in London. Where I'm from in Trinidad, carnival is a big thing with so much history, so I came up with the idea of bringing a taste of carnival to Britain as a peaceful way to showcase our Caribbean culture and bring the Caribbean community closer together. It *is* 1959 after all."

"1959!" Olivia whispered to Aniyah and EJ.

"That's over 60 years ago." EJ's jaw dropped.

"The carnival's on 30th January. Don't forget to add the date to the flyer, it's very important. When you're finished, we'll be off to see the carnival organisers."

By working together, the children managed to put the flyer together in no time. Claudia was impressed.

"It looks incredible! Aniyah and Olivia, take these notepads and pens and let's get our coats. You'll be interviewing members of the carnival committee for this issue of the newspaper."

The children grabbed their coats and followed Claudia down the stairs and out on to the street. She came to a halt at a bus stop.

"Here comes the 59," Olivia said.

"That's the one we need," Claudia replied.

They clambered aboard and found seats downstairs.

A woman in uniform with a machine dangling from her neck approached them from the front of the bus. It was a bus conductor.

Claudia explained to the conductor where she and the children were going and handed over some money. The conductor rummaged around in her pocket and then gave Claudia some change, before disappearing upstairs.

"A bus conductor?" Olivia whispered. "We don't have those now."

As the bus hurried on, Aniyah nudged EJ and pointed to a street sign that read "BRIXTON RD". "We're in Brixton! We have family here," said EJ.

But it wasn't the same. As the children stared out of the windows, they saw more boarded up windows and painted signs on the sides of buildings.

"Do you think having a carnival will *really* bring everyone together?" Olivia asked Claudia.

Claudia looked determined. "Yes, I do."

"Let me tell you about where I was born, in Trinidad," Claudia continued. "The French settlers brought their own festivals and traditions with them when they came to Trinidad, and the European settlers and free people of African descent held magnificent masquerade balls. Of course, the enslaved people on the island weren't allowed to attend these grand balls and instead, they'd watch through the windows.

Eventually the enslaved people began to throw their own festivals and celebrations during the burning and harvesting of the sugar cane, which is why it came to be known as 'canboulay' from 'cannes brûlées'."

"'Brûlée' means burnt in French," said Olivia.

"Exactly, 'burnt cane'," Claudia nodded. "And during canboulay, the enslaved people would mock their captors and dress up like the fancy French aristocrats, wear masks, then dance and sing to calypso music, a sound which developed from West African kaiso music."

Aniyah tried to imagine what the festival would've looked like. It sounded so different to Notting Hill Carnival.

"Calypso was a way for the enslaved people to communicate and, after they were freed from slavery in 1838, these celebrations got more elaborate and louder, a true symbol of freedom. The people in charge at the time didn't approve, so do you know what they did?"

"No, what?" asked EJ, leaning in closer.

"Oh, this is our stop," Claudia said. She bounded off the bus, and the others followed.

"What did they do?" EJ repeated.

"They banned music!" Claudia declared.

"No music!" Olivia grumbled. "Really?"

"Really. No drums, no singing in public and no masquerades." Claudia lifted her finger in the air in front of her and wagged it from side to side.

"That sounds awful," Aniyah cried.

"It was, and do you know what the people did? Why, they sang, they drummed and they danced!"

The children laughed.

"The people found a way to continue to celebrate. They used bamboo sticks and anything they could get their hands on to bang on instead of drums, like tins and other metal things."

"Tins?" asked EJ.

"Yes. Eventually some musicians noticed the different sounds the tin produced and began to experiment with big oil drums."

"Steel pan!" Aniyah blurted out, thinking about the steel pan orchestra she'd seen at Notting Hill Carnival.

"It's developed and changed over the years but that's how steel pan music came to be. The festival's also changed shape but at its heart, it's always been about bringing people together, opposing oppression, celebrating our culture and expressing oneself. I'm hoping that the carnival we're organising here can do the same."

"I have a feeling it will," smiled Aniyah. EJ and Olivia nodded in agreement.

The children followed Claudia as she slipped through a gate and into a small hall.

A steel pan band was rehearsing in a corner of the hall
and a woman was instructing a group of dancers in
the opposite corner.

"We use this centre as a meeting place to organise
the carnival," Claudia told the children.

EJ looked at Claudia. "I saw some more graffiti on
the wall outside," he said. "I think people should try and
get along, rather than fight."

"Exactly!" Claudia exclaimed. "Now, I want you to
interview the participants for the newspaper –" But before
she could finish, a voice cried out.

"Claudia! Come quick! Something terrible
has happened!"

Chapter 5

A man was beckoning to them. He looked worried.

"Allister, what's happened?"

Claudia followed Allister to a doorway off the main hall and the children ran behind them.

As they got closer to the door, their feet started to make a squelchy sound. Olivia looked down at the floor and saw a puddle of water.

Claudia and the children poked their heads through the doorway; the small room was flooded. The children could see fabric strewn in the murky brown water, and members of the carnival committee mopping up.

"It was a leaky pipe – the whole room flooded. Lots of the costumes have been destroyed!"

"Oh dear," Claudia rested her head in her palm. "There isn't much time to prepare new costumes for the television broadcast."

"Claudia, you told us the people in Trinidad didn't give up when the government said they couldn't have their festivals or their music. We shouldn't give up on the costumes!" EJ said.

Claudia thought for a moment. "You're right. Let's see what we can save."

EJ grabbed a mop and began to help the other committee members soak up the puddles.

Aniyah and Olivia pulled the wet costumes out of the water. Some of them were OK, and the girls laid them out to dry.

"Look at this one," Aniyah said, sadly. She held up a very long pair of trousers. "All the colour has run."

"Mmm, perhaps we can paint a new design on once they're dry," Claudia replied.

"This one's completely destroyed." Olivia pulled a wire, but whatever was attached to it before was now a mushy pulp.

"How about we reuse the shells and those strips of fabric?" Aniyah suggested, as she picked up another ruined costume.

"And the buttons and lace from this one?" said Olivia.

Claudia nodded. "Good idea. Give them to Sylvia and Patsy. They're piecing the costumes back together."

EJ put his bucket and mop down. "That's the water gone," he said. "What's next?"

"I still need you to take photos, EJ, and Aniyah and Olivia can interview people for the paper," Claudia replied. "Then we can all help piece the costumes back together."

EJ was excited, "I can't wait to use the camera properly. Uncle Lloyd showed me how to use a similar one."

"As well as interviewing everyone, how about we write about the flood and how we're all going to work together to save the costumes?" Olivia suggested.

Aniyah nodded. "That's a good story."

"I'll take some photos of the ruined costumes," EJ agreed.

Aniyah spoke to the musicians playing the steel pans.

"Come! You have a go," one of the musicians said. "Just find your rhythm!"

Olivia spoke to the dancers.

"This is a folk dance from Trinidad," one of the women told her.

They moved in time to the music and showed Olivia how to do some of the moves.

Aniya and Olivia wrote everything up in their notepads.

"This is great practice for *our* carnival," Olivia said.

Then they went back to Sylvia and Patsy to help remake the new costumes.

On the table there was a sewing machine, needles and different-coloured threads, glue, fabric and materials.

"I can't see any gems, glitter, Lycra or feathers," Aniyah said. "How are we going to make a carnival costume without them?"

Patsy opened her sketchbook and began to show the girls what they'd be working on.

"It looks like a sailor," Olivia said.

"It is!" Patsy smiled. "This costume started to appear in carnival when the British, French and American naval ships arrived on Trinidad's shores. The person wearing this costume comes from a family that's been dressing up as sailors for carnival, from generation to generation, since the 1880s. He's eager to show off this costume and showcase our culture."

All of a sudden, there was a pounding sound on the ground, getting nearer and nearer.

Chapter 6

A tall figure loomed over them. It was a stilt walker!

"Don't forget about me!" a voice cried from above.

"How could we? You're kind of hard to miss,"
Sylvia laughed. Aniyah had seen stilt walkers at Notting
Hill, and was in awe at their ability to balance, jump and
dance way up high, on thick wooden sticks.

"That's Clive, he's going to be the Moko," Sylvia said.

The children looked at each other. "The Moko?"

"It's another traditional mas character. The Moko's a protector; it's said that because he's so tall, he can see bad things before ordinary people can."

"He must wear those really long trousers we found!" Olivia laughed.

"Yes," nodded Patsy. "They're part of the Moko costume. We need to paint them and add some colour!"

The girls got to work, cutting, sticking and painting. With guidance from Sylvia and Patsy, the costumes began to come together.

When EJ had taken enough photographs for the newspaper, he got to work on the costumes too. They were joined by the committee members, the steel pan players and the dancers.

It was still dark when they finished gluing
the last piece of fabric onto the final costume.
When the children stood back to admire the work
they'd done, everyone cheered and clapped.

EJ handed Claudia the camera and Olivia
and Aniyah gave her their notepads with all
the interviews.

Claudia smiled and pointed the camera
at them. "You've been a big help. Let me take
a photograph of you."

"I thought carnival was just about
pretty costumes, good music and having
a laugh, but it's so much more than that,"
Aniyah said.

"And I just thought it was about
warm-crust chicken patties!" said EJ.

"It *is* those things," Olivia said.
"But it's also really important to
the community. I guess that's what
Winston meant."

49

As Claudia was called away by another committee member, a cloud loomed above the children.
A tornado that formed a wormhole appeared and pulled them in.

They arrived back in the basement of the restaurant. The Ludi board was still set up, just as they'd left it, and they could hear footsteps above, as everyone was still rushing around, organising things for carnival.

"I think we've done enough organising this year!" EJ said.

It was the big day; Notting Hill Carnival had finally arrived! The children eagerly got dressed into their carnival costumes, which were so different to the ones they'd been working on when they'd been transported back in time. Olivia was showing Aniyah the folk dances from Trinidad she'd learnt, when Aniyah's mum finally announced it was time to go.

Aniyah was enjoying herself, jumping to the music thumping out of the sound system, when she saw someone familiar. She nudged Olivia and said, "Look who it is!"

It was Winston, and he was dressed in the same fancy sailor costume Aniyah and Olivia had worked on when they'd been transported back in time!

"No way! The fancy sailor Patsy was talking about was Winston!"

When he spotted the children, he smiled and gave them a wave.

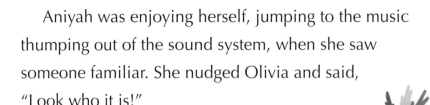

The children and Aniyah's mum waved back before continuing to play mas, a celebration of the old and the new.

Carnival Costumes Damaged

January, 1959

Carnival committee members were dismayed to find costumes had been damaged by water from a leaking pipe. With only a few weeks to go before the carnival is due to be televised by the BBC, a group of young volunteers worked tirelessly through the night to recreate each damaged item.

Claudia Jones 1915–1964

Claudia was born in Trinidad and Tobago and emigrated with her family to the USA.

A journalist and activist, Claudia moved to the UK and founded the first major black newspaper, *The West Indian Gazette*.

Claudia is often cited as one of the founders of carnival in the UK as she organised Britain's first indoor Caribbean carnival, the predecessor to Notting Hill Carnival as we know it today, which is now one of the biggest carnivals in the world.

Ideas for reading

Gill Matthews
Primary Literacy Consultant

Reading objectives:
- check that the book makes sense to them, discussing their understanding and exploring the meaning of words in context
- ask questions to improve their understanding
- draw inferences such as inferring characters' feelings, thoughts and motives from their actions, and justifying inferences with evidence

Spoken language objectives:
- maintain attention and participate actively in collaborative conversations, staying on topic and initiating and responding to comments
- use spoken language to develop understanding through speculating, hypothesising, imagining and exploring ideas
- participate in discussions, presentations, performances, role play, improvisations and debates

Curriculum links: Art and design; Relationships education – Respectful relationships

Interest words: shielded, lowered, browsing, ushered, shuffled

Build a context for reading

- Ask children to look closely at the front cover of the book. Explore their knowledge and understanding of carnivals. Discuss children's experiences of carnivals.
- Explore how the front cover image helps to understand what happens at carnivals.
- Read the back-cover blurb. Ask children what they think might happen in the story.

Understand and apply reading strategies

- Read pages 2–7 aloud, using appropriate expression.
- Explore children's understanding of what has happened and who the characters are in this first chapter.
- Discuss what the children now know about carnivals. Explore how they think the main characters are feeling about Notting Hill Carnival.
- Give children the opportunity to read the rest of the book.